A
Working
Holiday

a novella by

F. M. Cipriano

FMC Press

A Working Holiday

[ISBN 978-0-9941743-8-3]
First published 2018 by FMC Press
PO Box 13179
Law Courts VIC 8010
Australia
Copyright © F. M. Cipriano 2018
Book Cover Design: Rachmad Ridwan
Editing: Delia Thornton of The Expert Editor

A catalogue record for this
book is available from the
National Library of Australia

This book is a fact-based fiction. Names and characters are
the product of the author's imagination or are used fictitiously.
Any resemblance to actual persons, living or dead, is
coincidental. No responsibility can be accepted by the publisher
or author for any damages resulting from the misrepresentation
of this work by associating any resemblances to any factual
person, living or dead. All care has been taken in the preparation
of the information herein, but no responsibility can be accepted
by the publisher or author for any damages resulting from the
misinterpretation of this work. All contact details given in this
book were current at the time of publication, but are subject to
change.

Published by FMC Press

www.fmcpress.com

Table of Contents

About the Author

F. M. Cipriano (Frank) was born in Melbourne, Australia. He has a Bachelor of Business, a Graduate Diploma in Accounting and a Master of Taxation.

Frank was a career public servant with the Australian Taxation Office (ATO) until he gained a voluntary redundancy, departing on 29 August 2014.

Since leaving the ATO, Frank has pursued his passion for writing. His other published books are: *A Bachelor's Travels*, *My Taxing Career* and *White Man Dreaming*.

A Working Holiday is a novella inspired by an overseas working holiday Frank embarked on in 1988, which provided him with a myriad of new adventures, opened his mind to new perceptions and taught him important lessons about human nature.

Other Books by the Author

A Bachelor's Travels

Roland is a single, 27-year-old public servant who lives with his parents. He enjoyed life until most of his mates got married, which results in a solo overseas trip that triggers a lifelong obsession. He wanders the globe, through the continents of Europe, Africa, Asia and the Americas. His journeys range from painstaking itinerant travel to the serendipity of spontaneous adventures, involving a plethora of unique experiences that enrich his knowledge, augment his appreciation of different cultures, impact his attitudes and uplift his spirits. However, approaching middle age, Roland feels it may be time for his overseas travels to come to an end. Is it time to open a new chapter in his life and settle down to a comfortable existence in Australia? It is a question he wrestles with until circumstances ultimately decide his course.

Other Books by the Author

My Taxing Career

Fred Campari had no intention of being employed by the Tax Office but ironically, that's where he ended up. He developed a liking for his work and concerted his efforts to make a positive difference; however, he was constantly stymied and frustrated by the actions of senior management. The Tax Office seemed to have developed a culture that encouraged and rewarded backstabbers, informers and lackeys. In fact, these qualities appeared to be prerequisites to staff advancement. Fred eventually resigned himself to the fact that he had reached the peak of his career but he had not bargained for a possible fall when an attack by senior executives would threaten his very survival.

*   *   *

"When I was a kid, I was asked what I wanted to do when I grew up. I replied that I wanted to join the circus. Oddly enough, by joining the Tax Office, I sort of did."

Fred Campari

Other Books by the Author

White Man Dreaming

The completion of a law degree and job offers from a number of law firms should have been a graduate's crowning achievement; however, Art Costello meets it with indifference.

Art broods over his future before deciding to take a couple of gap years. Once committed to pursue other endeavours, he becomes hopeful that he may discover some meaning to his life. But he doesn't anticipate that it will lead him to evaluate his very existence.

Art gains knowledge about a people considered to have the oldest continuous culture on the planet, to have the world's longest living art tradition, and who remain true to their spiritual beliefs, since the time of creation, through their enduring connection to each other, to nature and to all living things.

And yet these very people have been subjected to the most atrocious injustices ever perpetrated against human beings.

Art learns a great deal from them, but the greatest lesson he learns is that of survival.

These are the Indigenous peoples of Australia.

Chapter 1

A Vacation Quandary

The computer science graduates of 1982 were eagerly looking forward to their university's 10th anniversary reunion.

John Pesce and Con Psarris were particularly excited as they were also approaching their 10th year anniversary at work, which would trigger long service leave of 90 days leave at full pay.

Con and John immediately hit it off as freshmen at university, which surprised the other students as they were opposites in almost every way.

John was of average height, was widely popular, with an above average IQ, while Con was short, unattractive and, even though it was universally accepted that he was a computer programming whizz, many thought he was a nerd.

The only similarities the pair seemed to have was their rhyming first names and the fact that their surnames—'Psarris' in Greek and 'Pesce' in Italian—both translated to 'fish' in English.

An added similarity emerged three years later when, after completing their university degrees, they both gained employment at the same computer software company.

Con and John set off for the reunion together, with John driving.

"So, do the two of you still keep in touch?" asked one of the graduates.

"Yeah, we do," Con replied. "In fact, we see each other almost every day."

"We see each other on weekdays as we both work for the same company," John was quick to clarify.

"You guys aren't gay, are you?" another graduate asked.

"Of course not!" Con barked back.

"No, we're not gay," John confirmed. "We're more like brothers."

*   *   *

Con and John excitedly discussed their respective vacation plans.

"I'm keen to travel to Europe and meet my relatives in Greece," Con stated enthusiastically. "But I don't think I have the spondulas," he added with a sombre tone.

"I also plan to travel overseas," John advised in an upbeat voice. "But I don't have the money to go to all the places I wish to visit," he added with resignation.

Over the next few months, they often raised their international travel plans and compared notes.

One day, John presented his proposed itinerary to Con who was highly critical, although he failed to come up with any original ideas of his own.

"My plans involve a six months working holiday," John advised.

"Why are you bothering to go to work?" Con automatically enquired — his common, kneejerk reaction as he often sought clarification for the obvious.

"I'll work for a few months in London," John explained. "So with the money I save, plus the prepayment of my annual leave and long service leave, this should provide me with enough money to travel to all the destinations I want to visit and allow for a great overseas holiday."

"Work in London?" Con queried. "What makes you think you'll be able to find a job in London?"

"C'mon, Con," John urged. "Don't you recall how many of the other graduates mentioned how there was a high demand for computer workers in London and how easy it was to find a job?"

"Yeah, that's right," Con said, and then reflected on the idea before he responded with his usual catch-cry. "By George, I think we've got it!"

Chapter 2

Going Abroad

John took a cab to Melbourne International Airport, arriving well ahead of time. He checked in his luggage before he sat down to arrange his travel documents. He was filling out his departure card when he heard a ruckus and looked up to see Con enter the terminus with an entourage.

John sat back to observe the group of a dozen or so people circling Con as if he was a rock star.

As the group paraded towards the check-in counters, John recognised Con's mother, father and two sisters, but had no idea who the other people were.

Con's mother was in tears as, one by one, the group members wished Con a bon voyage.

Con's father was consoling his wife when John considered that it might be an appropriate time to reveal himself. As soon as he did, the group erupted once more.

"Hey look, John's here!" Con's father declared as the group cheered. "See, there's no need to worry; John will take care of your son."

Con's mother held out her arms as she approached John, still crying.

"It's okay Mrs Psarris," John said as they hugged. "Everything will be alright and your son will get to meet your family in Greece."

John hoped his last comment might provide Con's mother with some comfort; however, the mention of her family, whom she had not seen for many years, caused her to wail and cry with increased intensity.

"There, there," John said as he continued to hug her and pat her on the back while he looked over to Con and his father, who both opened their palms, shrugged their shoulders and returned wry smiles.

When emotions subsided, Con fell into the line to check in, the group following him as he progressed in the queue.

After Con checked in, there was another round of emotional goodbyes.

John and Con managed to extricate themselves from the group and they made their way to immigration.

They took their seats in the plane and the engines soon started. A rumble reverberated around the cabin, which raised their level of excitement and they exchanged broad smiles.

Con had a window seat, and John the aisle seat. As the plane took off, Con's eyes were glued to the views outside his window. He continually slapped John on the shoulder and pointed out the views. With each slap, John looked out, nodded, and politely grinned.

It was about 15 minutes into the flight when John eventually piped up. "Alright!" he asserted. "You don't have to slap me every time you see something."

Thirty minutes into the flight, John was asleep when he was woken by mouth snapping noises. He looked over to observe Con munching on his dinner. He then looked in front of him and saw that his tray table was stowed and he had no food.

"Why didn't you wake me for dinner?" John queried.

"You said you didn't want to be disturbed," Con replied.

John gave Con an angry stare and frowned before he hit the call button for attendance.

*   *   *

The plane touched down at London Heathrow and John led Con through to immigration. John made it through expeditiously, although he had to wait a considerable time for Con.

"How come it took you so long?" John asked Con when he languidly appeared.

"I don't know," Con responded. "The guy kept on asking me all these stupid questions."

"Like what?" John pried.

"What are you here for? Where's your passport? What accommodation do you have in London? Do you have a return ticket? Do you have proof of funds available to you over the period of your stay in England?"

"I was asked the same questions," John advised, incredulous. "They're all standard questions."

"Well, I still think they were stupid," Con opined.

"I know who's stupid," John quipped.

They caught the train to Victoria Station and weaved their way through the crowds to the taxi rank. Their eyes widened as they saw a long line of classic London black cabs and were thrilled to jump into the back seat of the next one in the rank.

It was late Friday afternoon and the city

was producing a cacophony of blaring noises emanating from the streets abuzz with people and congested with traffic.

The cab ride through central London featured many of the iconic and historical landmarks.

Con and John were bouncing around on the back seat as they twisted and turned from one side of the vehicle to the other, rubbernecking to capture views of all the attractions.

"We've arrived," the driver announced as the cab came to a halt in front of their hotel.

The duo settled into their twin-share room, both exhausted by their flight.

"I'm absolutely shot," John admitted. "I think I'll hit the sack."

"Yeah, I'm pretty-well stuffed too," Con said. "I think I'll do the same."

Chapter 3

Settling into London

Early Saturday morning, John armed himself with his city map as he prepared to set off on his walking tour of London. He was rummaging through his luggage for his camera and the noise caused Con to wake up.

"What are you up to?" Con asked, emitting a drowsy yawn.

"I'm getting ready before I set off to do some sightseeing," John replied.

"So what should I do?" Con asked.

"Whatever you want," John said, exasperated. "You can join me if you want."

Con raised his upper body from his bed and rubbed his eyes. "Yeah, I think I'll do some sightseeing too."

They headed off and travelled the length and breadth of central London on Saturday, finishing their assault on the main attractions the following day.

Fatigued by their weekend activities, they hauled themselves out of bed on Monday morning and were off to seek out longer-term accommodation for the balance of their three-month stint in London.

They inspected a number of places, ranging from basic hostels to shared apartments. They concentrated their search around Earls Court, as it was a popular haunt for Australians. They were unsuccessful in finding anything so they placed their names on waiting lists for apartments and hostels in central London.

They returned to their hotel and changed into business suits. John had a list of professional recruitment agencies and set off to go job hunting. As usual, Con just tagged along.

They visited a number of job agencies, but none of them were very optimistic. The recruitment agents responded with a common theme, "We can place your name on our lists, but we can't promise you anything."

It was now Wednesday and they had only two more days paid up at their hotel. John was downbeat, but Con didn't seem too concerned.

"It will all work out in the end," Con reassured.

Later in the day the phone rang and John promptly answered.

"Hello, is this John?"

"Yes it is."

"We have a shared apartment available for you and Con," the female real estate agent advised in a shrieky voice.

"Oh, that's great," John exclaimed. "Where is it?"

"Ealing."

"Ealing?" John repeated. "Where's that?"

"It's in west London, just outside central London, but it's easily accessible via the Underground on the Piccadilly line."

John placed his hand on the telephone transmitter and checked with Con, who just shrugged his shoulders. John frowned before he communicated his decision. "We'll take it."

On Sunday afternoon, Con and John checked out of their hotel and caught the train to Ealing Common Station. They then trudged a couple of blocks to the four-bedroom apartment.

There was a commotion as John knocked on the front door. The sound of the knock caused the ruckus from within the apartment to die down.

After a couple of minutes, the door slowly creaked open and a young man's head popped out. "Can I help you?"

"We're supposed to be moving into the apartment today," John advised.

"Oh, really," the man responded. "I thought it wasn't until Monday."

"No, it's today," Con confirmed, without actually knowing whether this was the case.

"Well, come in. I'm Jessie," the man said as he fully opened the door. "And the other tenants are Jordan, Sheila and Rhonda," he advised as he pointed them out respectively.

There were around a dozen people in the apartment and John reflected on the situation before he spoke. "So are there a total of six tenants?" John asked. "Because I thought there was a limit of four people to the apartment."

"The lease does allow for up to four people," Jordan said. "However, we count a couple in a room as one person."

John scrunched up his face, expressing incredulity to the contention.

"We've checked with the real estate agent and they said this was fine," Jessie added.

John was still unconvinced. "Really, well I might just confirm this with the agent."

Con and John settled into their rooms while the commotion recommenced. It wasn't long before the festivities developed into a full-blown party.

John made his way into Con's room. "I can't believe this," John said.

"Yeah, I know," Con retorted. "There's hardly enough storage space."

"Very funny," John said. "I don't fancy staying in these surroundings with non-stop partying.

"It's the weekend," Con pointed out. "I'm sure things will settle down during the week."

Chapter 4

Enter the Park

The following week, the chaos in the apartment continued every day unabated. John was most upset when he visited the real estate agent and briefed them of the matter.

"The situation sounds very unpleasant and we will try to do everything we can," the professionally dressed female real estate agent advised in a blasé fashion. "However, the landlord works in Germany and when we previously brought up these issues with him, he seemed unwilling to take any drastic action. He seems content as long as the tenants don't cause any major damage and they keep on paying the rent."

"If that's the case, Con and I will be looking to move out as soon as possible."

Accommodation in the central London area at a reasonable price was proving difficult to find. Further, Con and John were still looking for work.

Con didn't seem too perturbed with their predicament but John was very worried.

It was Wednesday morning when the apartment telephone rang.

"Did you say you wished to speak to John," Jordan said, after he answered the call.

John was making his way towards the telephone when Jordan continued.

"Oh, sorry, you wish to speak to Con."

John knocked on Con's door as he called out, "Con, there's a telephone call for you."

Con exited his room and strutted to the telephone.

"Hello. What? You have accommodation for me? That's great," Con said spiritedly and took down the details of his new abode.

Con was about to hang up when John rushed over and waved his arms to get Con's attention. John then pointed to himself and whispered. "What about me?"

"Is my friend John Pesce on your list?" Con asked. "Oh, no John. Okay."

Con was ecstatic as he got off the telephone and returned to his room.

John followed him. "So what's the deal?" John asked.

"I've got accommodation at a hostel in central London and can move in any time within seven days," Con advised. "I'm paid up here until Saturday so I can move next Sunday. It's perfect."

"Yeah, perfect," John replied in a disconsolate voice.

John returned to his room, closed the door and flopped on his bed. He was most upset as he lay on his bed when he heard the telephone ring again and he eagerly sat up.

"What? You want to speak to John," Jessie

said after he answered the call. "Oh, you want Con, just a minute."

John was overwhelmed with disappointment as he overheard Con speaking on the telephone.

"Hi, this is Con. What? I've got a job? That's great!" he exclaimed as he wrote down the details. "Yes. I can start first thing Monday. That's perfect."

John listened intently to hear whether Con would enquire about him or whether his situation was brought up in the conversation, but there was no further discussion and Con hung up.

John collapsed prostrate on his bed. *I can't believe it*, he thought. *I do all the organisation and all the work and yet Con gets all the opportunities. I just don't get it.*

*   *   *

John spent the rest of the day moping around the apartment while Con was packing and the other tenants were continuing with their usual festivities.

The next day—Friday—Con set off to inspect his new accommodation while John continued with his sightseeing around London.

John returned to the apartment in the late afternoon and relaxed on his bed. He heard the telephone ring and he unwittingly reacted with an ironic smile.

"What, you wish to speak to John?" Jordan said after he answered the telephone.

John was expecting to hear that the call was actually for Con, before Jordan continued. "Okay, I'll get him for you."

John hesitantly raised himself from his bed as he heard a knock on his door.

"Hey John, are you in?" Jordan called out. "There's a telephone call for you."

John slowly opened his door and walked over to the telephone as if he was in a daze.

"Hello, it's John speaking."

"Hi, I'm a receptionist from the Park hostel and we have a placement for you. If you're interested, you can check in any time over the next seven days."

"That's fantastic!" John exclaimed and took down the details. "It's odd as my friend, Con, received a call from the Park the other day and, while he gained a placement, they advised him that there was nothing for me."

"That's probably because we have a few receptionists with separate lists and you must be on a different list."

"Oh, I see," John said. "Thank you."

*　　*　　*

Con hadn't returned to the apartment, so John stepped out and had dinner at an Indian restaurant, followed by a few drinks at a pub.

John arrived back at the apartment late in the evening and found the door to Con's room closed so he went to bed.

Waking up Saturday morning, John prepared himself for more sightseeing. He walked to Con's room and noticed that the door was still closed. He knocked but there was no response. He opened the door but Con was not there.

The other tenants had gone away for the weekend and an eerie silence fell upon the apartment.

John spent the whole day exploring the parks and gardens around London, including Covent Garden. He enjoyed the day and celebrated on his own, with a meal and drinks at a pub.

Returning to the apartment Saturday evening, John noticed that Con's door was still closed. He knocked on the door but there was no answer. He then opened the door to find it vacant. Con had apparently moved out.

*   *   *

John finalised his packing on Sunday morning and set off for his new accommodation in the early afternoon.

There was a flurry of activity at the Park's reception.

"Hi, I'm John and I believe you have a

placement for me."

"Oh yes, you're the guy who's sharing with Biff. Fill out this form. Here's your key. Biff's not in at the moment, but you can move into the room."

"I thought that I might be sharing with my friend Con," John said.

"Con's temporarily in a single room until permanent twin-share accommodation can be organised," the receptionist advised. "He's lucky as he's enjoying a single room at the price of a twin-share room."

That'd be right, John thought.

John made his way to his twin room on the second floor. It was a very basic, small room cramming in two single oak beds and two matching cupboards with mirrored doors. John's bed was spaced from the wall to fit in a cream-coloured, cast-iron heating radiator, which was placed under a matching cream, double-hung timber window. There was a communal bathroom at the end of the floor.

John was settling into his room when a

young man entered. The man had light brown hair, green eyes, a large gap between his two front teeth, and was wearing a goofy smile.

"Hi, you must be Biff."

"Yeah, and you must be John."

"That's right."

"Have you heard anything about me, John?"

"No why?"

"Oh nuffin'. You're Australian, aren't you?"

"Yes, I am."

"There are a couple of other Australians at the Park; I can introduce you if you like?"

"Sure, that'd be great."

"Hey Marty!" Biff shouted as someone was passing by.

"Yeah Biff," a young man replied as he entered the room.

"This is a new guy at the Park and he's Australian."

"Hi Marty, I'm John."

Marty was short and lean, with a mop-top

haircut, and hailed from the Northern Territory.

"Hey Marty, where's Lizzie," asked Biff.

"Dunnow, but she might be in the TV room."

"Come on John, let's check it out."

Biff, Marty and John scurried down the stairs to the basement television room.

Marty introduced John to Lizzie—a young woman with green eyes and red hair—from Perth.

"By the way, John," Biff continued, "this is Poppy."

Poppy was a young woman with blue eyes and blonde hair, from Ireland.

"We're going for dinner," Poppy immediately mentioned. "You should join us."

"That'd be great," John replied. "Hey, you wouldn't happen to have come across a friend of mine named Con?"

The group members looked at each other and appeared reluctant to respond, although

Biff was undeterred. "You're friends with that moron?"

"He's not a moron," John replied. "He's just a bit of a nerd."

"I guess that's why he's hit it off with Harold," Marty stated. "Harold's very nerdy."

"I'm going to pick up my girlfriend," Biff interrupted. "So I'll meet you there."

Lizzie, Poppy, Marty and John headed off for dinner, taking the Underground to Chinatown.

Arriving at the Wong Key Restaurant, they climbed the stairs before they came to a halt ahead of a queue lined up between the second and third floors.

"What's the hold up?" John asked.

"This is the Wong Key," Marty replied. "It's got four levels of seating and it's usually packed. It must be the most popular restaurant in London."

"The food must be good," John guessed.

"No, the food's pretty average," Marty replied.

"But it's damn cheap," Lizzie added.

They had advanced slightly in the queue when Biff arrived with his girlfriend Gema—a young, attractive Spanish woman with deep brown eyes and long, wavy brown hair.

"We've got a bit of a wait," exclaimed Biff, continuing the banter with whoever was close enough and in any way responsive.

The establishment was very noisy and chaotic as the group were eventually led to a table.

"Where are the bleedin' menus?" Biff yelled.

The menus appeared out of nowhere and, after a short respite, the waitresses were calling for orders. It wasn't too long before the food was served. The eating was voracious and the discussion lively.

After they downed their last morsels of food, the waitresses presented the bill and began wiping down the table.

"What about dessert?" Biff retorted with a big cheesy grin and then proclaimed, "It's time for an ale!"

It was a short stroll to a pub where there was an amateur comic on stage. After his act, he approached the group. "Hey Marty, how goes it?"

"Good thanks Bill, this is John from Australia."

"Blimey, not another bleedin' Aussie," Bill quipped.

After a number of drinks, the group called it a night.

"Where are you going John?" Poppy queried.

"To the Underground," John replied.

"We don't take the Tube at this time," Poppy advised. "We take the bus."

They arrived back at the Park in the early hours of the morning. John was exhausted and welcomed his newly acquainted bed for a good night's sleep.

Chapter 5

First Day at Work

Waking up late on Monday morning, John looked over to Biff's bed to observe that it was made up. He checked the time and was disappointed to realise that he had missed out on the included breakfast.

John was yawning and stretching out in bed when he recalled that he needed to advise the recruitment agencies of his change of address. He quickly dressed and sped downstairs to use the public phone in the reception area.

"Fortunate you rang John," a perky sounding woman from one of the recruitment agencies exclaimed. "We have a placement for you. If you can make it to our office sometime today, you should be able to start tomorrow."

"Yeah sure, thanks," John replied excitedly. "I can be there within the hour."

John was absolutely elated; with long term accommodation and now a job, everything was finally falling into place.

Fronting up for the interview at the recruitment agency, John was provided with details of his placement by a young female agent with long blonde hair and hazel eyes.

"I believe my friend named Con Psarris obtained a similar placement," John mentioned at the end of the meeting.

The agent checked the records as she brushed away a ringlet curl of hair that was trailing over her face. "Yes that's right and he's due to commence today."

"I assume your firm distributes separate lists to different agents to handle the various placements," John suggested.

"That's right, how did you know that?"

"Lucky guess, I suppose."

*   *   *

Returning to the Park, John was surprised to see Lizzie and Poppy.

"I thought you two were working today," John said.

"We're both very sick," Lizzie replied. "We've got Mondayitis."

"It's very contagious you know," Poppy added with a smile. "We're going to enjoy the beautiful day and you should join us."

Poppy, Lizzie and John wandered the streets and roamed around Kensington Gardens under glorious sunshine before they checked out a few of the shopping stalls down Portobello Road.

John's thoughts were on his first day of work, so he returned to his room to organise himself and get some early shut-eye.

John woke up early Tuesday morning after a sound sleep. He looked over to Biff's bed and it was still made up.

Does this guy ever sleep here? John thought.

John shaved, showered and went down for breakfast. It was a cafeteria style buffet with a reasonable selection. He enjoyed his meal, as he did the beaming smiles of the women servers who were from various parts of Britain and continental Europe.

Dressed in his conservative grey business suit, John grabbed the brolly he had purchased in Portobello Road; it was the first umbrella he had ever owned. He set off for the Underground and caught the central line train to Bank Station, in the heart of the business district.

John had little trouble finding the heritage building that housed the firm—the Corporations Data Group. He took the elevator to the second floor and approached the reception counter.

"G'day. I'm John, and I was sent by the recruitment agency to report to Mr Gordon Flash."

"Okay, I'll let him know you've arrived."

John observed the slim, young receptionist push her ergonomic office chair away from her desk, stand up and proceed down the corridor. She had long, straight, dark-brown hair with a blunt-cut fringe. She was wearing a tight fitting white shirt that had the two top buttons undone, revealing a teasing glimpse of the contours of her petite breasts. She also wore an exceptionally tight black skirt with a slit in the back. The ensemble was completed with a pair of glossy, black, high-heeled shoes. The tight get-up restricted her movements so that she could hardly walk, and caused her to waddle; her stilettos giving off loud, staccato, knocking sounds as they echoed off the floorboards.

The receptionist turned into a side doorway and was out of sight when the sounds of her stilettos ceased for a few minutes before they recommenced.

John then observed the receptionist returning alongside a middle-aged gentleman wearing a double breasted, navy-blue suit, white business shirt and gold coloured tie.

As the man approached John, he extended his arm and they shook hands.

"Good morning John, I'm Gordon Flash."

"G'day, pleased to meet you."

"If you could follow me into my office, we can have a chat."

Gordon collected a couple of files from the receptionist before he led John down the corridor to his office.

"Take a seat John."

"Thank you, Sir."

"You may call me Gordon."

"Thanks, Gordon."

"I thought I'd meet up with you personally as you are starting a day later than a group of nine operatives that commenced yesterday," Gordon explained. "The Corporations Data Group is a start-up firm that is to provide information on corporations around the globe. The information will ultimately comprise statistical and diagnostic data, which will require computer programming and software architecture skills. However, at this stage you will be required to simply input accounting and economic data into our computer systems. So that's basically it for now. Do you have any questions?"

"No, that all sounds clear."

"Very good. I'll show you around."

Gordon escorted John via the elevator to the third floor, which was an open office area with rows of workstations occupied by staff on computers.

John ran his eyes over the group and noticed Con.

"Good morning everyone, this is John Pesce and he'll be joining the group," Gordon announced. "I'm sure you'll make him feel welcome."

The group members were looking at John with expressions of indifference; however, Con looked startled.

John looked over to Con, smiled and waved. Con turned to his monitor and continued working.

"I'll arrange for someone to give you a rundown of the procedures," Gordon advised. "In the meantime, you can settle into the spare workstation."

John walked over to Con's workstation. "Hi Con, it's good to see you after such a long time," John joked. "What's it been, four days?"

Con looked up and rolled his eyes.

"What's your problem?" John asked.

"I can't believe that you moved into the hostel and then got this job and you never let me know."

"I never had the chance," John explained. "I tried to catch up with you at the apartment and the hostel, but you weren't around and our paths didn't cross."

"Well, I think you intentionally avoided me because you were jealous that I managed to score accommodation and a job when you didn't."

"That's not true."

A young, petite woman with frizzy, sandy-blonde hair made her way to Con's workstation.

"Hi Con. Hello John, my name's Sissy. I'm one of the operatives here and I've been instructed to give you a rundown of the procedures."

"That'd be great," John replied.

Sissy made her way to her workstation while John took a moment to look down at Con, who was ignoring him.

John shook his head and made a snapping sound with his mouth before he made his way to Sissy's workstation.

Chapter 6

The British Groove

Con left work early, saying farewell to a few of the staff but without saying goodbye to John.

As John was leaving the office, he was joined in the lift by Sissy.

"Do you know Con, do you?" Sissy asked.

"Yeah, we go back years to our university days. He's a good friend," John replied.

"A good friend?" Sissy queried. "Most of the staff find him a little strange."

"I guess he is a little unconventional but he's harmless, and a guru when it comes to computer programming."

Returning to the Park, John bumped into Poppy in the reception area who was with an obese, cross-eyed, middle-aged man.

"Hi John, this is Harold. He's a long-term resident who's lucky enough to have a single room," Poppy advised. "A few of us are meeting up in the foyer to go to the pub if you wish to join us."

"Sounds good," John remarked. "I've had a long day and I could do with a drink."

"I hear you're from Australia," Harold said. "I'm from Birkenhead in Merseyside, you know, 'ferry cross the Mersey'," he sang.

"I know the song well," John commented. "Will you be coming to the pub?"

"Noouu. I don't like pubs," Harold replied. "I prefer to watch television."

John returned to his room and dressed down, before passing by Con's room. He knocked on the door but there was no answer, so he proceeded to the foyer.

Poppy, Lizzie, Marty and John went to a

local pub where a number of residents from the Park mingled, although Con was not there.

Poppy filled John in on the gossip and the different cliques within the Park. She also gave him a rundown about Biff.

"Biff was expelled from university for various forms of misconduct. He was kicked out of a hostel in Yorkshire due to fighting. He also had a run-in with his former roommate at the Park, who didn't appreciate Gema's sleepovers, and they had a bit of a disagreement on other matters," Poppy explained. "However, you shouldn't have to worry about the sleepovers anymore, apparently they go elsewhere and Biff has been warned; he's on his last life at the Park."

"Well, it must have been a stern warning," John said. "I hardly ever see him."

"Don't count your chickens before they're hatched," Lizzie commented, "as he often comes and goes in waves."

"So what's the story with Con?" Marty

asked.

"Con and I went to university together and we've been friends ever since," John advised.

"You're friends with Con?" Poppy queried.

"What's wrong with that?" John asked.

"We just find him a little weird," Lizzie said.

"I guess he does come across as a bit strange and maybe a little slow, but he's alright," John reassured. "And he's a genius when it comes to computer programming."

After another long session at the pub; the gang called it a night. The first few days at the Park set the tone for the next few months. John soon realized that the exhaustive extra curricula activities were to be the norm, and the pub scene was to be a daily event. It was a routine that he didn't mind in the least.

*   *   *

The following morning, John was at breakfast when Con made an appearance. Con went to the breakfast counter, collected a tray and cutlery, selected his food and grabbed a cup of coffee.

John looked on as Con moved past a number of occupied tables, proceeded past a couple of unoccupied tables, and took a seat on his own. John shook his head as he picked up his tray and walked over to him.

"I'm not going to ask if I can sit here," John stated as he rested his tray on the table and took a seat.

Con ignored him, continuing with his breakfast.

"You know you could have made an effort to see me over those few days, like I did with you," John said, although Con continued to ignore him. "Or maybe you did try to catch up with me but I wasn't around and our paths didn't cross."

Con put on a sourpuss face and continued with his breakfast, not saying a word.

John pursed his lips. "Oh no, don't tell me. You actually didn't try to see me because you felt so smug in scoring accommodation and a job that you felt superior to me and couldn't be bothered with me."

Con looked up with a startled expression. "I did try to see you."

"But I wasn't around, right," John added.

"That's right," Con confirmed.

"Which is exactly what I did," John exclaimed as he raised both arms in the air. "Hallelujah, the truth has set us free."

Con cracked a smile as he shook his head. They then finished breakfast and travelled to work together.

*   *   *

John developed a close relationship with Poppy, Lizzie and Marty. They spent every day together, and on weekends they would either go on day excursions around London or take long weekends, travelling around different parts of Britain.

Con followed his usual tendency of tagging along.

Harold edged his way into the group,

where he made intermittent appearances. He was permitted on the day excursions, but the women were not prepared to have him on any overnighters as they couldn't put up with him, nor did they trust him.

Chapter 7

Ceremony of the Keys

Harold knocked on John's door late Saturday morning.

John rolled out of bed and cracked open the door.

"Helloouu John," Harold said in a melodious tone. "I've got tickets to the Ceremony of the Keys."

"Ceremony of the Keys, what's that?"

Harold's eyes opened wide as he recounted the story of the tradition.

John was engulfed with details about the ceremony involving the exchange of the keys at the Tower of London that had taken place every day for several hundred years, except for one day during World War II.

"That's fascinating, Harold."

"Precisely, and, as I've said, I've got tickets."

"Well that's great Harold; I'm sure you'll enjoy it."

"I would like you, Poppy and Lizzie to come too."

"Sure, I'd love to come. What about Poppy and Lizzie?"

"I hoped you would ask them for me."

"Sure, I don't mind," John said. "I'm catching up with them this afternoon."

Later that day, John met up with Lizzie and Poppy. "Hello ladies, have I got a treat for you."

"What's that?" Poppy queried.

"Harold's got tickets for the Ceremony of the Keys and he'd like us to join him."

"Oh that," Lizzie remarked. "He's already asked us and we said no."

"Really, that old sod," John commented. "No matter, you can say yes now."

"Why should we?" Poppy asked.

"It actually sounds pretty historic," John suggested.

"Terrific," remarked Poppy sarcastically.

"Come on, I'd really like to go and it'd be so much better if you two come too," John insisted as he put on a puppy-dog eyes expression.

The women frowned, then eked out smiles and finally relented.

It was a chilly London evening when Harold and entourage rolled up for the ceremony, which had amassed a crowd of between 40 and 50 people.

A guide provided an historical background as Harold lent forward and appeared at the ready to take over at any stage.

There was the sound of rustling, followed by loud stomping as soldiers pounded the pavement in their heavy boots, marching in perfect time before coming to an abrupt stop.

After a few moments of deathly silence, there was a loud cry. "Who goes there?"

People almost jumped out of their skin in fright, but all remained quiet.

"The keys," was the return cry.

"Whose keys?"

"The Queen's keys."

John watched Harold standing erect with pride as the loud sound of a trumpet echoed around the gathering.

As the ceremony wound up and they exited from the Tower gates, Poppy, Lizzie and John all burst out with laughter.

"Why are you all laughing?" Harold interrogated.

There was continued laughter for a while, until it slowly died down.

"I'm sorry," Poppy eventually replied. "But during the ceremony I couldn't help picturing every household in the country doing their own little ceremony of the keys every night."

"And why are you laughing John?" Harold questioned further.

"Oh, nothing really," John stated. "But I just couldn't help thinking that after hundreds of years, they'd know whose bloody keys they were."

Chapter 8

Land's End

Con and John were in the basement television room when Poppy and Lizzie made an appearance.

"What are you guys up to?" Poppy pried.

"We're discussing various options for weekend holidays," John advised.

"How come you haven't included us?" asked Lizzie.

"We didn't think you'd be interested," Con replied.

"Maybe we are interested," suggested Poppy.

"Well, you're welcomed to join us," John offered.

"So, where are we going?" Lizzie asked with a grin.

After an exhaustive debate about possible travel destinations, they didn't make too much headway, although they did agree that they needed to categorise their attractions in geographic areas and that their first main objective would be to visit Land's End.

Poppy and Lizzie volunteered to book the accommodation and John agreed to book the rental car.

Con had no tasks assigned, although he was very vociferous in putting forward his views, and was all smiles.

On Friday 1 April 1988, which was the Good Friday holiday, John picked up the car—a Fiat Uno—in the early afternoon and drove to the Park.

Poppy, Lizzie and Con were waiting for him in the foyer and jumped for joy at his arrival.

"Couldn't you find anything smaller?" Con asked sarcastically.

"It's the only model they had left on such short notice," John replied.

"Is it going to be big enough for all our luggage?" Lizzie asked.

"We're only going for two nights," John said. "So you shouldn't have too much to bring."

Poppy and Lizzie both looked at each other and bolted up the stairs.

John and Con retrieved their bags and waited a considerable time before the women arrived.

Con insisted on taking the first stint of driving and John took the front passenger seat to do the navigating. The women were seated in the back seats, separated by their rather sizeable pieces of luggage.

After driving a few blocks, Con remembered that he needed to put on his spectacles. Even though it improved his vision, it didn't seem to improve his driving.

It took almost an hour for Con just to get out of greater London. He missed the turnoff from the M25 motorway to the M4, as he was adamant that the most direct route to Plymouth was via the M3. It was soon after they past Winchester that Con became flustered by the road signs, his frustration soon erupting into infuriation.

"I told you that the M3 led to Southampton," John commented.

"If we'd taken the M4, we would have ended up in Wales," Con retorted.

"The M4 does lead to Wales," Poppy interjected. "That's why we would have taken the M5 turnoff."

They took the opportunity to have dinner at a pub near Southampton before they continued.

Con handed over the driving to John and, as he refused to move from the front seat, Poppy navigated from the back seat.

It took them a total of six hours to reach their bed-and-breakfast in Plymouth, arriving at 10.00 pm. They had a leisurely walk around town before they hit the sack.

Early Saturday morning they enjoyed breakfast at the hotel before setting off. Con refused to drive, so it was left to John.

They travelled through Penzance and straight on to Land's End.

As soon as they found a car park, they ambled over to the coast to survey the rocky shoreline. They admired the deep-brown cliffs, contrasting against the blue of the open seas; the constant rolling waves fringed by white foam. The sights were augmented by the celestial view of puffy, white, cumulus clouds in an otherwise bright blue sky.

They observed the Longships Lighthouse off the coast and then focused further out to spot the Isles of Scully, 28 miles away.

They breathed in the salty sea air as a cool breeze kicked up, refreshing their faces. The cold caused Poppy to zip up her jacket and tighten her scarf, while Lizzie grasped the edges of her coat and wrapped them around her waist.

They walked over to a sign post that read *John O'Groates 874*, highlighting the distance of 874 miles from the most northerly land tip of mainland Britain at John O'Groates to the most southerly tip at Land's End.

They took turns taking photos, the last shot being a group photo where John set the timer and ran over to his position, falling over the top of the others.

"I think we should take another shot," Lizzie suggested.

They then headed to Penzance where they had fish and chips for lunch.

Continuing on, they took the most direct route along the coast, passing through Falmouth, St Austell, Liskeard, Plymouth, Exeter, Dorchester, Bournemouth, Southampton, and Chichester. They stopped at Brighton for dinner and had a walk along the beach before driving the short distance to their bed-and-breakfast in Lewes.

First thing after breakfast, they drove

directly to the Battle of Hastings, scene of the 1066 battle between King Harold II of England and William Duke of Normandy—William the Conqueror.

They explored the site and the abbey ruins before they drove to Hastings, where they walked through the old town and popped into the Shipwreck Museum.

They were admiring the exhibits when they came across an English family—mother, father and young son.

"The British sailing ships travelled the world, even as far as Australia," the father commented, pronouncing Australia, "Ostralia."

The boy looked up to his father. "It's not Ostralia, Daddy, it's Orstralia."

John and Poppy turned to each other.

"Posh kid," Poppy said, and they both laughed.

The group proceeded through Folkestone and on to Dover, where they had a quick photo stop at the white cliffs before they drove on to Canterbury.

They visited the famous Canterbury Cathedral before dinner and then strolled around town. Returning to the car, John was about to jump into the driver's seat.

"I'll be driving back to London," Con declared.

"That's fine by me," John replied. "It's straight through on the M2 motorway."

"I know," Con said. "And I expect to see road signs of London all the way."

Chapter 9

A Day at the Races

The following week was consumed with excited discussion about the Grand National steeple chase.

John and Con sought to procure interest for an outing to the great race. Lizzie and Poppy were invited but they declined, as they considered horse jumping races to be deplorable.

Agreeing to avoid the hassle of driving a rental car, they booked an all-day bus tour instead.

On Saturday 9 April 1988, John boarded

the bus and took a window seat towards the front.

Con got on, walked down the aisle past John, and took a window seat towards the back of the bus.

John turned his head with a quizzical expression as he stared at Con.

Returning his stare, Con smiled and waved.

People got on board at regular intervals.

A young woman walked down the aisle, looking from side to side, and stopped near John. She then looked down the bus before she took the aisle seat next to him.

The woman had brown eyes and long, dark brown hair. She wore blue jeans and a dark green puffer jacket.

John looked over at her but she looked straight ahead. "Hi, my name's John," he said.

The woman looked at him. "Hi, I'm Joan."

John detected an Australian accent. "Where are you from?" he asked.

"I'm from Brisbane. And you?"

"I'm from Melbourne. Are you travelling

alone?"

"Yeah, I am. My friends were supposed to come but they pulled out at the last minute." Joan said with a frown. "You?"

"Oh, I've got a friend but he sat down the back of the bus."

"Why isn't he sitting with you?"

John didn't respond but just shrugged his shoulders. Joan smiled.

The final passengers took their seats, with the last person seated being the driver who soon started the engines and slowly pulled away.

"And they're off," John commented, imitating a race caller, and Joan laughed.

As they progressed towards Aintree, Joan and John engaged in continuous conversation, which reached a crescendo as they arrived. When they alighted the bus, they recommenced their conversation.

Con disembarked and followed them for a short distance before he sped up to catch them. John introduced the two and the trio proceeded to the racecourse entrance.

They had a few hours before the big race. None of the three were interested in betting on any of the earlier races, so they took their time to walk around parts of the course and enjoy the carnival atmosphere.

As the time for the race neared, they inspected the horses in the parade ring before they considered their bets and rushed off to lay them.

"So what did you go for?" Con asked Joan.

"Bucko at 12 to 1," was her succinct reply. "I just liked its name."

"What about you, John?" asked Con.

"I went for Monanore at 28 to 1," John advised. "I just liked its look."

"And you Con?" Joan asked.

"I went for the standout horse, Brass Change."

"Why do you say it's the standout horse?" John asked. "It's 100 to 1."

"It's a standout because it's the only grey horse in the race."

"Oh, I thought I saw two grey horses," Joan revealed.

"What?" Con exclaimed.

"Yeah, there's another grey, it's called Smith's Man and it's 33 to 1," John added. "Gee, it'll be a pity if it wins."

"Blast, I'll have to back that one as well," Con said with a scrunched up face and he headed straight for the bookmakers.

When Con returned, they went trackside and debated where they should position themselves.

They eventually agreed to stand on the Canal Turn for the first lap and Becher's Brook for the second. They shuffled around near the Canal Turn and settled into position.

A public address announced that the best turned-out horse was Bucko.

"Your horse won!" John commented to Joan and she rolled her eyes.

The horses lined up and the starter soon sent them on their way.

"And they're off," John announced,

imitating a race caller once again. Joan laughed, as she did the first time, although this time with an exasperated sigh.

There was shouting and cheering as the horses came to the first steeple and the crowd fixed their eyes on the jump, seemingly more interested to see whether any horses fell rather than which were leading.

The immediate aftermath resulted in three horses falling, including Sacred Path, the favourite.

Proceeding down the straight, the horses tackled the series of jumps. They came over Becher's Brook, with two more horses falling.

"There's only one grey horse, number 34, that's Brass Change," Con observed. "What's happened to the other grey horse?"

"Well, I think we all know the answer to that," John said.

The amplified sounds of the pounding of horses' hooves and the cracking of jockeys' whips signalled their approach. This was followed by loud thrashing sounds as the horses jumped and crashed through the birch fences at the Canal Turn.

The remaining horses continued on in the gruelling race, urged along by their jockeys. As they completed the first lap, Joan, Con and John edged their way toward Becher's Brook.

They keenly viewed the horses make the jump as the leading horse—Strands of Gold—came down, as did another horse towards the rear of the field.

"My remaining grey horse is still in the race," Con declared excitedly. "Although it's well back in the field," he added in a downtrodden tone.

"I saw number 12," Joan remarked. "So Bucko's hanging in there."

"Number 14 is still there," John advised. "So Monanore is hanging in there too."

The field was reducing, with the remainder struggling on. Over the 27th fence three horses refused to jump, two fell and two pulled up.

"My grey's down!" Con yelled with

disappointment.

"Bucko's down too," Joan added with resignation.

"What about yours?" Con asked John.

"I don't know," John replied, perplexed.

Over the last and the race caller identified Durham Edition taking over the lead from Rhyme 'N' Reason followed by Monanore.

"Your horse is third," Joan shouted, exhilarated.

"Oh, what!" Con added, seemingly upset by the news.

"My horse might run a place," John said in a blasé manner, trying to contain his excitement.

The race caller described the concluding stages as Durham Edition leading on the far side but with Rhyme 'N' Reason on the near side challenging again. Monanore was hanging on.

As they came to the line Rhyme 'N' Reason won, second was Durham Edition and Monanore finished third.

"Hooray, your horse came third," Joan rejoiced.

"You won and we lost," Con said sombrely. "You're the only one to collect some winnings."

John smiled with the joy of picking a place getter, but this was dampened by the facts of the post-race statistics. Out of 40 runners that started, only nine horses completed the course.

This isn't a horse race, John thought. *It's more like Russian roulette.*

"Let's join the crowd and check out the jumps," Joan said in an upbeat voice.

Joan darted onto the track and Con quickly followed.

John took a moment of contemplation and then perked up before he went in their pursuit.

"Bloody hell," Con cursed as he approached Becher's Brook on the landing side. "This thing is as high as I am."

"What's that?" John responded. "Five foot

nothing."

"I'm five foot six, if you don't mind," Con snapped back in a deep, grainy voice.

"How in the hell did those people get on top of the fence?" Joan asked.

"They climbed up from the other side, where the ground is higher," John replied, as he made his way to the top of the fence and sat down.

"Hey, I can take your photo," Joan offered.

John handed over his camera and Joan took a couple of shots. Joan and Con then scrambled up the fence to join John and someone obligingly took a group photo of the three of them.

They caught the bus back to London, amongst an atmosphere of heated post-race discussions. At the end of the drive, Joan exchanged contact details before she parted ways.

Chapter 10

The Midlands

The next day, Lizzie proposed an outing to Greenwich. Poppy, Marty and John were keen but Con was not.

"It's hardly worth my time to visit a place that's only famed for simply happening to be the location of Mean Time," Con remarked.

They left early Sunday afternoon by train. It was a sunny day and they leisurely meandered their way through Greenwich market to the Cutty Sark, which found its home at a permanent dry dock. They looked from side to side to appreciate the grandeur of the

British clipper sailing ship, before taking glimpses of the stunning views of the River Thames and the city of London.

They moved on, passing the University of Greenwich and the National Maritime Museum, finding themselves in front of the Queen's House. They admired the facade of the building before they entered to view the decorative interior containing artworks and galleries.

They grabbed a bite to eat before they visited the Old Royal Observatory.

After exploring the observatory, each took their turn at standing over the Meridian Line, placing one foot on either side of the line—east and west. Marty was the last to assume the stance.

"I hazard to think what part of your anatomy is over zero degrees longitude," John remarked.

"I can tell you," Marty replied. "It's my crown jewels."

They all broke out into laughter as they

walked onto the expanses of Greenwich Park and lay down on the lawn. They used their naked eyes as observatory instruments to scan the blue skies dotted with small, puffy clouds.

After some time spent relaxing and dozing, they made their way back to the Park hostel where they bumped into Con.

"So was Greenwich worth the trouble?" Con asked them.

They looked at each other before they cross-fired their replies.

"Absolutely."

"It was great."

"Fantastic."

"I wouldn't have missed it for the world!"

Con examined their expressions, trying to gauge whether they were joking, but he couldn't tell. "Maybe I'll go there," he replied. "One of these days."

*　　*　　*

Early the next week, John called upon Poppy and Lizzie to gauge their interest in a getaway for the long weekend, to take advantage of the Monday May Day bank holiday; however, the women weren't interested. He then visited Con, who was still enjoying the luxury of his single room.

"I'm so lucky to have a single room all to myself," Con bragged. "And I'm only paying the price of a twin-share."

"I've been lucky too," John countered. "I've hardly seen Biff since I moved in."

"Where are the girls?" Con queried.

"They're not interested in going anywhere this weekend."

"So, where are we going?" Con asked.

"We've done southern England so I was looking to nearby destinations to the north. I've been thinking about the Midlands," John proposed. "Is that okay?"

"Whatever," was Con's curt reply.

"I thought we could pass through Cambridge, along the east coast, through Norwich and King's Lynn and on to Lincoln, where we can spend the night. We can then head west through Nottingham to Liverpool, returning via Stratford-Upon-Avon and Oxford back to London."

"What's in Stratford-Upon-Avon?" Con queried.

"It's the birthplace of William Shakespeare and a well preserved medieval town," John explained.

"That sounds reasonable," said Con.

"Do you want to book the rental car or the accommodation?" John asked.

"I really don't want to do either."

Con's response was not unexpected to John and he felt that it would be fruitless to try to persuade him to do something.

"Very well," said John. "I'll do both."

On Saturday morning, John picked up the car and drove to the Park where Con was waiting for him.

"I'll drive," Con insisted, and he took the wheel.

Con experienced his usual difficulty getting out of London and it was almost midday by the time they arrived in Cambridge.

They had lunch before strolling around the quaint town where they took in the tranquil surrounding of the Backs Park, inspected the various edifices of learning, and enjoyed the sweeping views along the banks of the River Cam.

John took over the driving and they proceeded to King's Lynn. They stopped for a walk about the town, visiting St Nicholas Chapel, King's Lynn Minster and The Walks—the city park.

Moving on, they arrived at their guest house in Lincoln. After settling in, they indulged in a pub meal before retiring.

Early morning, they visited Lincoln Cathedral and the imposing Lincoln Castle.

Con wasn't interested in taking the wheel, so John continued driving. They moved on to Sherwood Forest, where they headed straight for the visitor's centre.

They obtained information and a map before setting off on their desired walk, their destination being the Major Oak—Robin Hood's hideout, as the tale goes.

They weren't far down the trail when Con started complaining, "We're in the middle of nowhere. Where in the blazes is this tree?"

"We've only been walking for five minutes," John said. "It's supposed to take 10 to 15 minutes."

It did, in fact, take between 10 and 15 minutes for them to reach the Major Oak, but this didn't stop Con from complaining. "This thing looks as though it's going to collapse at any minute."

"I'd like to see what condition you'd be in after 800 years," John joked. "You wouldn't be sprouting out of the ground at all; you'd be six foot under."

John and Con made their way back to the car, admiring the scenery along the way.

Con still wasn't interested in driving, so John took the wheel again.

They continued to Nottingham, where they visited the cathedral and the hilltop castle.

Their next destination was Liverpool—the home of the Beatles—where they had accommodation booked for the night.

They retired to their room and John was suggesting a plan for the morning activities in Liverpool when Con came up with the brainwave of visiting Blackpool instead.

"Why do you want to go to there?" John asked.

"It's often talked about," Con replied.

"I agree that it's often talked about," John said, "as the butt of many jokes."

"Well, I want to go and that's that," Con insisted.

John expected that Con would never budge, so he relented.

In the morning, they drove to Blackpool with John urging Con along to visit the Blackpool Tower and the South, Central and North Piers.

John was heading back to the car when Con pulled him up.

"I want to spend more time at the piers,"

Con declared.

John made no attempt to resist. He simply turned around and escorted Con back to Central Pier.

"I'm going to check out a few of the attractions," Con said.

John took a moment to collect his thoughts before he responded. "Okay, but don't take too long. As soon as you've finished, we'll meet back here."

They set off on separate paths to explore the carnival atmosphere that featured games and rides.

It looks like a fun place, John thought. *For juveniles.*

John returned to the meeting place and waited a while before he became restless. He then walked up and down the pier in search of Con, but there was no sign of him.

Where in the blazes has this guy gone? John thought.

After a while, John walked up and down the pier again and there was still no sign of

Con. He returned to the meeting place and Con was nowhere to be found.

Maybe he's returned to the car, John wondered and, losing his patience, he walked back to the vehicle.

Con was not at the car and John began to fret. *Should I go back to the pier or should I stay here?* he thought. *He'll eventually have to return to the car so I better stay put.*

John sat in the car for what seemed to be an eternity. He was becoming increasingly worried when he saw a familiar figure strutting down the road.

When Con made it to the car, he opened the front passenger door, got in and slammed the door shut.

"What in the hell are you doing here?" Con yelled.

"I looked all over for you and waited at the meeting place but you weren't there," John explained. "So I eventually decided to return here."

"You were supposed to wait at the meeting

place!" Con shouted.

"I waited a long time," John countered. "And you weren't there."

"You were supposed to wait!" Con retorted.

John made no further statement. He started the engine and drove. They proceeded in complete silence, ignoring each other. They headed, via Birmingham, to Stratford-Upon-Avon.

"Why are we stopping here?" Con queried.

"It's William Shakespeare's birthplace, remember?"

"So just read his works."

"I've done that," John said. "I only want to visit his birthplace and the grave where he and his wife, Anne Hathaway, are buried, at the Church of the Holy Trinity."

They visited the attractions under further remonstrations by Con. When they got back to the car, Con expressed his desire to drive.

Con sped off and looked straight ahead as he followed the road. As they approached

Oxford, he drove on, bypassing the town.

"We need to take the turn-off for Oxford," John pointed out.

"Oxford," Con cursed. "We've done enough for this trip."

"But we agreed that we'd include Oxford."

"You can do Oxford some other time," Con stated as he continued on to London, looking smug and with John wearing a frown the whole way.

Chapter 11

It's Football

It was a fine, sunny Saturday morning on 7 May 1988 when Marty noticed John walking on the opposite side of the street.

"Hey John, this is Jack, my Kiwi mate, and we're off to the footy to see whether Chelsea can avoid relegation," Marty shouted out. "Do you want to come?"

"Sure," John replied. "I haven't been to a soccer game in London."

"Football, John," Marty corrected. "It's called football."

They caught the district line train to

Fulham Broadway Station. The train was absolutely packed and at every station there was a surge of people trying to get on. Things were manageable before a frail, old woman tried to get off.

Oh no, John thought. "Excuse me, a lady is trying to get off!" he yelled, as he endeavoured to heave his body weight against the crowd.

Marty, Jack and a few other passengers attempted to do the same, but to no avail.

There was a bit of a scuffle and the woman was trembling, fear written all over her face.

There was general concern among passengers that the woman might miss her stop, as well as a growing fear for her safety.

Out of nowhere, a colossus of a man emerged from the crowd. He looked like a football hooligan complete with football garb, tattoos and body piercing. He raised his arms and cried out, "Make way you mindless beasts!"

What happened next was almost biblical.

The crowd parted like the Red Sea and the woman walked through, uninhibited.

After the woman left the train, the crowd returned to its previous calamity. Marty and John looked to each other in disbelief.

John then uttered, "That guy's Moses."

Arriving at Fulham Road, they made their way to Stamford Bridge and the Chelsea Football Ground where there was a large crowd, singing and chanting.

"Back in Melbourne I follow the Carlton Football Club in Australian Rules football and they're known as the Blues," John stated. "As Chelsea is also known as the Blues, I might go for them."

"The fans in England take their football fairly seriously and we're going into the visitors' area with the Charlton supporters," Jack advised. "I suggest you'd be better off not going for either side."

They entered the ground and found a position marginally less crowded. The ground was not at capacity, but it was still abuzz with barracking and singing.

At the kick-off, the animation and noise level picked up another few notches.

The game was not of a high standard, but its importance justified the tense and excited atmosphere.

Before long, Chelsea managed to squeeze in a goal. The home side lifted in unison with a mighty roar and went berserk.

Several Chelsea supporters jumped the partitioning fence that separated the home supporters from the visitors and it was on for young and old.

The disturbance was some distance away from Marty, Jack and John but the punch-up soon spread like wildfire. In an instant, police emerged, apprehending the infiltrators and it was over as quick as it had started. They were flabbergasted.

Attention was back on the game and, soon after, Charlton equalized with an emphatic goal.

Oh no, John thought. *What now?*

Fortunately, there were no further disturbances and the game ended. With a one all draw, Chelsea was to be relegated.

It was some time after the match, but the visitors weren't moving.

"What's going on?" John queried.

"They vacate all the home supporters before they let the visitors go," Jack explained.

It got to the point where the home side of the ground was empty and the visitors' side of the ground was still occupied.

The remaining crowd stood amid an eerie silence.

John was gazing above the walls of the stadium, imagining the possibility of darts or Molotov cocktails coming over the top at any moment.

The gates finally opened and the crowd became mobile. They were led out by mounted police in what seemed like a military operation, with foot police lining the streets on both sides and mounted police leading the crowd.

Marty, Jack and John were escorted all the way to the train station, where they had to endure another crowd crush on the train ride home.

Chapter 12

Visiting Castles

Following an invigorating day at the football, John was comfortable joining Poppy, Lizzie and Harold on Sunday for a more sedate outing to Hampton Court Palace.

Con was invited but declined the opportunity. "I don't think it's worth visiting a place just because it happened to have been the residence of King Henry VIII," he reasoned.

The train journey to Hampton Court Station took under an hour. After disembarking, they traversed the Hampton

Court Bridge to Hampton Court Palace.

They wandered through the corridors and peeped through many of the various rooms, halls, chambers, galleries and the chapel, where they viewed numerous historical artworks, paintings, furniture and military arms.

As they emerged from the palace, the open expanses of the Great Fountain Garden and Hampton Court Park—Home Park—came into view.

"These gardens are truly breathtaking," Lizzie sighed, to which Poppy, Harold and John agreed.

Harold enthusiastically led the group as they strolled through the gardens.

Exhausted by the day's activities, they returned to London for a late evening dinner before retiring to bed.

*   *   *

The following weekend, Poppy, Lizzie, Marty and John planned to visit Windsor

Castle on the Saturday and Leeds Castle on the Sunday.

Con wasn't interested in either, without giving a reason, and Harold declined because he was going home to Birkenhead for the weekend.

They took the train to Windsor Castle, which took under an hour.

They walked briskly to make the most of their time and commenced by planning their attack on the castle, with the aid of a map.

Even though they moved at a fast clip and limited their tour to the major attractions, they checked the time to realise that it took them almost four hours.

"And they reckon to allow two to three hours," Marty commented.

As they left the castle they were in animated discussion of the many highlights.

"So what did you like the best?" Marty asked the others.

"I simply adored Queen Mary's dolls," Lizzie immediately declared, which was understandable given her fetish for dolls.

"No, no, it would have to have been St George's Chapel," Poppy was quick to opine, which was reconcilable given her religious bent.

"I thought the State Apartments were the most impressive," John said, which could be rationalised on the basis of a process of elimination as he had less of an interest in dolls and religion.

"What about you?" Lizzie asked Marty.

"I was inspired by all of it and I think Charles II was successful in his quest to rival the Palace of Versailles," Marty posited.

"I didn't know you'd visited Versailles," John said.

"I haven't," Marty advised. "But I couldn't imagine anything more impressive than Windsor Castle."

*　　*　　*

On the Sunday, Lizzie, Poppy, Marty and John jumped on a coach from Victoria Station to Leeds Castle.

It took almost two hours to arrive and they all limped off the coach and stretched their limbs before proceeding to the castle.

They explored the castle in quick time, about an hour, and checked their watches. It was only 11.30 am, which gave them three and a half hours before their return coach ride.

They had a bite to eat before they explored the grounds. They were relaxing on the lawns when they volunteered their thoughts.

Lizzie went first. "I liked the Dog Collar Museum; it was something different and I like dogs."

Poppy was next. "I was impressed by the Gatehouse Exhibition that captured the development of the castle's history."

"I appreciated the overall grandeur of the imposing stoned castle," John said. "What about you Marty?"

"Leeds Castle is reputed to be the loveliest castle in the world," Marty noted. "But I think

Windsor Castle was prettier."

Chapter 13

Lakes and Dales

Poppy and Lizzie were keen to join Con and John on their next weekend holiday, as the destinations were the renowned areas of the Lake District and Yorkshire.

Con wanted to drive and, with a great deal of navigational assistance, managed to take the direct route to the medieval city of York, which took four hours with a single stop along the way.

They had a bite to eat before they climbed Clifford's Tower, situated high on a mound that provided panoramic views of the old city.

They moved on to visit York Castle Museum, housed in 18th century prison buildings, where they viewed the various galleries and exhibitions.

They walked through the York Shambles, observing the timber-framed houses and buildings while peeping through the shop windows.

They stumbled upon the Museum Gardens and were thrilled to discover the ruins of St Mary's Abbey.

They arrived at the York Minster and visited the cathedral, as well as the historic treasures and collections.

They concluded their tour of York by scaling the old city walls and walking along the ramparts, enjoying the views.

Con handed the keys to John to drive and they proceeded to their next port of call, the city of Newcastle, where they settled into their accommodation before stepping out for dinner.

"I'll be driving tomorrow morning," Con announced during dinner.

"Do you want to drive for any particular reason?" Poppy enquired.

"I'll be seeking out Hadrian's Wall," Con advised.

The others looked at each other, seemingly mystified by what Con meant, and shared expressions of concern. It was an uneasiness that troubled them throughout the night.

After breakfast, the group left Newcastle with Con taking the wheel. He travelled east, on the lookout for signs, but he could not spot any. He turned off at a couple of side roads but was still unsuccessful in locating any remnants of the wall. He then started to become frustrated.

"Based on what I've read, there are two main locations that feature ruins of the wall, Heddon-on-the-Wall and Housesteads," John said.

Con was unresponsive and continued driving until he saw a sign, which happened to be Heddon-on-the-Wall. He turned off.

They located some ruins of the wall, which was enough to satisfy Con.

Returning to the car, Con announced that he didn't want to drive so John took the wheel. He drove on until he saw a sign to Housesteads and turned off.

They viewed the ruins of a Roman fort before they continued to the Lake District and checked into their accommodation at Ambleside.

They spent the rest of the day exploring the Lake District and dining in the town of Windermere.

"I'd have to say, the Lake District has some of the most colourful and spectacular scenery I've ever seen," John said during dinner. "The colours are so contrasting and vivid."

"Have you ever been to Ireland?" asked Poppy.

"No I haven't," John admitted.

"You should check out the scenery there," Poppy suggested.

The next day, they continued to explore more of the Lake District, partly driving and partly walking.

They feasted at the town of Keswick before proceeding to the Yorkshire Dales National Park.

They followed a couple of the nature walks, appreciating the wide open spaces and the fresh, invigorating air.

They had a meal in Sheffield before making the long journey back to London.

"I'll be driving," Con stated, seemingly having developed an obsession for driving in and out of London.

Chapter 14

Wales

Poppy and Lizzie were highly excited as the weekend approached, which was a long weekend due to the Spring Bank Holiday on Monday 30 May.

They would be travelling to Wales, accompanied by Marty and John. An added attraction for them was that Con and Harold wouldn't be going.

Marty took the first stint of driving. He needed no navigational assistance as he effortlessly drove out of London and on to their first stop at Stonehenge.

After parking the rental car, they sauntered to the prehistoric monument under the veil of a cloudy sky. They walked around the site, admiring the ring of stones standing approximately two metres high and one metre wide.

"It really is a strange place," Lizzie remarked.

"Which fits in with its mysterious past," Poppy commented.

"A mysterious and mystical past," John added.

They moved on to the city of Bath and initially drove to the Bath lookout.

"It's a pretty cool city," Marty said.

"You can say that again," Poppy added. "In fact, I think it's captivating."

They spent some time enjoying the panoramic views before they left, driving a little way and parking the car close to the city centre.

They walked via Royal Crescent, which boasted a curved row of terraced houses featuring fine examples of Georgian architecture. They then stumbled across a Georgian garden, which they were pleased to wander through before they visited Bath Abbey and moved on to the Roman Baths.

"These baths are so well preserved," Lizzie remarked as she paced herself behind the crowd, continuously looking every which way.

They proceeded to the terrace and looked down onto the Great Bath where the turquoise waters contrasted against the orange and brown colours of the stone columns and paths. They circled the terrace and then descended the stairs.

They inspected the Sacred Spring, the Temple Courtyard and the East Baths before they returned to the Great Bath at the lower level.

"This place is truly amazing," Poppy remarked.

"It's more impressive than I could have imagined," John said.

They made their way back to the car and

drove on, crossing the Severn Bridge over the River Severn to Cardiff, the capital of Wales.

They had lunch and walked about the capital before driving on to Swansea, where they stopped for a drink and a wander about the coastal city.

They travelled west to Fishguard and then followed the coastal road to Aberystwyth for their overnight stay.

After breakfast, they continued up the coast to Caernarfon where they were blown away by the imposing view of Caernarfon Castle.

They traversed the moat and entered the castle where they were in awe of the mighty fortress.

There was much activity inside, which happened to be a re-enactment of medieval sword-fighting.

They climbed up the towers and walked along the walls, taking in views of the city and sea.

They stayed in Caernarfon for lunch before

continuing along the coastal road, all the way to the picturesque walled city of Chester in England.

By the time they parked the car and walked to the town centre, the heavens had opened up.

They took cover under rows of verandahs of black and white Victorian buildings set among well-preserved medieval edifices. They took the opportunity to inspect the shops while the showers persisted.

When the rain cleared, they enjoyed a meal in the town and then drove to their overnight accommodation.

They woke up early for breakfast ahead of their return drive. Marty took the wheel and it was a smooth drive all the way back to London.

Chapter 15

Another Day at the Races

Con and John went to work on Tuesday and then had the day off on Wednesday 1 June, to attend the Derby at Epsom Downs.

They took the train from Victoria Station and a shuttle to the racetrack. As soon as they entered the course, they commenced studying the form guide.

"What are you going for?" Con asked John.

"I really don't know based on the form," John advised. "I might examine the horses and go on looks."

They viewed the horses and made their way

to the bookmakers.

"What horse did you pick?" asked Con.

"I couldn't pick anything based on looks," John replied. "But I'm going to back Minster Son at 7 to 1 for no particular reason."

Con referred back to his form guide. "I can't get anything out of this," he said. "I might just go for the grey horse, Sheriff's Star, at 16 to 1."

They placed their bets and found a place along the rails of the race track.

"My word, the grey horse is getting fractious behind the barrier," John noted. "It just kicked out! Did you see that?"

"Yeah I did," Con said. "If it gets scratched at least I get my money back."

"Oh look, they're placing a blindfold on it," John remarked.

"Bloody hell," Con commented.

Sheriff's Star was placed in the barriers, as was the rest of the field. The gates opened and a mighty roar erupted from the crowd.

"Oh no, they forgot to take the blindfold

off," John quipped.

"Oh what!" Con yelled.

"I was just kidding," John admitted.

"You bastard," Con said. "Where's your horse?"

"I think it's mid-field."

"The grey's well back," Con noted disappointedly.

The horses made their way around the track with two furlongs to go.

"Where's your horse now?" Con asked John.

"Still mid-field and doing nothing," John said. "But look at the grey, it's on the extreme outside and running on strongly."

"Hey yeah, it is," Con called out. "Go Sheriff's Star, go Sheriff's Star!"

The horses were flat out as they rounded the home turn and made their way down the straight to the finishing post. While Sherriff's Star made a stirring sprint, it died on its run.

"Sheriff's Star didn't win," Con said with resignation. "It finished sixth."

"Oh well, at least it finished, which is better than the two greys you had in the Grand National."

"Very funny," Con said. "Where did your horse finish?"

"My horse had a very even run as it was mid-field all the way," John advised. "I think it finished eighth."

"Well at least my horse finished in front of yours."

Chapter 16

Finishing Off the Job

John enjoyed his work at the Corporations Data Group. He was given freedom to manage his own time, he could work as many hours as he desired, and he had a good relationship with Gordon and his co-workers.

On the other hand, Con managed to get on the wrong side of most of the staff and was testing the patience of Gordon, who had already warned him of his lack of professional behaviour.

After a group work lunch on Friday, where a number of ales were consumed, Con returned to work, got into a disagreement with one of the male staff and verbally abused him in front of Gordon. This proved to be the last straw.

"I'd like to see you in my office, Con," Gordon directed.

Gordon walked towards the elevator and Con followed. A bell chime and the lighting up of the red down-arrow signalled the lift's arrival. As the elevator doors closed, both Con and Gordon faced forward. Con had a glazed facial expression, his eyes fixated on John.

John continued with his work, although his mind was preoccupied with concern for Con.

After half an hour, Con emerged from the lift escorted by a security officer. He walked over to his desk, collected his briefcase, and left the building.

John left work soon after, rushed back to the Park and knocked on Con's door.

After a few moments, the door slowly came ajar. Con allowed the door to swing open as he drifted back to his bed, where he took a seat.

"Are you alright?" John asked as he entered the room and closed the door.

"Yeah, I'm fine," Con replied.

"So what happened?"

"Gordon said something about my conduct being unacceptable and that my services were no longer required."

"That's too bad," John said. "What are you going to do now?"

"Now that's a real dilemma," Con replied, scratching his head.

"You can always check with the recruitment agency to see if you can get another job," John suggested.

"Another job? Hell, I don't want another job," Con revealed. "My dilemma is whether I take a tour to Scotland or Ireland."

"Sorry, what do you mean?"

"Well, Gordon actually did me a favour and things have worked out great," Con explained. "I planned to give Gordon two weeks notice, which would have been the proper thing to do; however, I decided that I'd had enough and I was going to leave next week. By relieving me of duty, I get to leave straight away."

"That's fine, but that'll cost you money. Have you saved up enough for your travels?"

"More than enough," Con boasted. "We estimated that we needed to work about 12 weeks for 40 hours a week at around six pounds an hour. We've already worked 10 weeks at eight pounds an hour for an average of 50 hours a week so I've already saved what I need for my trip to Greece."

"Well, that's okay then."

"It's better than just okay," Con continued. "When Gordon gave me notice, he also gave me an extra two weeks pay. So with the extra money and extra time, I can now afford a tour. But I still have the dilemma."

"That being?" John asked.

"Should I go to Scotland or should I go to Ireland? Hell, I might even do both."

John was dumbfounded.

Chapter 17

Bongos with a Bang

John was a heavy sleeper, but his usual condition was being disturbed some nights by the strange noises emanating from the room next door.

The noises emitted a variety of notes and pitches that caused him to be continually woken up.

The noises ranged from sounds of nature, jungle noises and animal sounds with accompanying music featuring bongo drums.

John raised the matter one night at the pub and it was greeted with an uproar of hilarity from the other residents at the Park.

"The practices of the mystery woman have been the subject of much gossip over the years," Poppy advised.

"I've heard she's the longest-term, permanent resident," Lizzie said. "Although most people have never even seen her."

"She must come and go through some secret passage," Marty suggested. "I've heard of guys who have been on watch to spy on her, but she never made an appearance."

"Well, I've never seen her," John admitted, "but I always hear those bloody bongos going off."

"I don't think that's the only thing going off," Harold said in soliloquy, although his words were heard by everyone.

"You sly fox," Marty remarked. "What is it that you know that you haven't told us?"

"Oh nothing," Harold replied, teasingly.

"Come on Harold," Lizzie urged. "What is it that you're keeping secret?"

A broad smile emerged on Harold's face;

seemingly lapping up the attention, but he would not be drawn into divulging anything.

"I think I know what it is," Poppy said. "I think the mystery woman is a bit of a nympho."

The crowd erupted in uproar, with many expressing a reaction.

"No way!"

"The mystery woman has been playing hide the sausage."

"She's been given the bone."

"She's been riding the flagpole."

"She's been having her bearded clam speared."

"Settle down guys," John urged. "We really shouldn't jump to conclusions."

"Why don't we adjourn to John's room one night for a few quiet drinks and nibbles to see if we can make out what's going on?" Marty suggested.

"That's a brilliant idea," Poppy said.

"That's spying," Harold exclaimed.

"You don't have to join us if you don't

want to," John said.

"Oh no," Harold replied. "I'll be there."

*   *   *

The group convened around 9.00 pm on Sunday evening in John's room. The attendees comprised Poppy, Lizzie, Harold, Marty, Con, John and several other residents from the Park, with everyone supplying drinks and snacks.

They had been quietly partying, drinking, eating and joking for almost an hour but there was no sign of activity from the adjoining room.

"I don't think anything is going to happen tonight," Harold said.

"I agree," Con was quick to add. "Tonight is going to be a fizzer."

After another hour, the group began grumbling, fearful that the night would be uneventful.

"Did you hear that?" one of the residents whispered.

The group was silent but not a sound was heard, so they assumed the resident had imagined the noise. The group considered whether they should abort the gathering when faint noises were heard.

"What's that?" Marty asked.

"It sounds like noises of nature," Poppy said.

The group could detect the sounds of running water, whispering wind, rustling leaves and chirping birds.

They moved around to get more comfortable and settle into their positions. They then concentrated and listened acutely.

The sounds were rising in volume as classical music was introduced. The music started faintly but soon rose in volume. As the music got louder, animal noises came in followed by bongo drums. Finally, distinct heaving and moaning sounds were heard, although it was difficult to determine whether they were animal or human. The various sounds culminated into a crescendo that reached a tremendous and abrupt climax.

The group looked at each other, their eyes wide open, bewildered, in complete silence.

After a while, Poppy broke the silence. "Wow, that was amazing."

"Yeah, amazing," Marty agreed with a smile. "In fact, I think I came in my pants."

Chapter 18

A Night Out

It was past midnight on Saturday morning and John was fast asleep when he was woken up by a loud bang.

"What in the hell!" John shouted.

"It's only me," Biff advised as he paced around the room.

"I haven't seen you for ages. What have you been up to?"

"I had a falling out with Gema," Biff explained. "Everything was going great until recently. I wanted sex but she didn't. I don't know what her problem is. It's not as if she has to do much; she just has to lie there."

"You can't be serious," John said as he shook his head. "What about considering her feelings?"

"I'm done with her," Biff declared. "It's Friday night, so let's hit the clubs."

"You can go," John responded. "I'm too tired to go clubbing."

"What's wrong with you? Get up and we can go and have a great night out."

"Forget it, Biff. I've had a hard week, I'm tired and I'm too comfortable in bed."

"You sound like an old man. Get out of bed and we'll hit the town."

"No, no way."

"Don't be a bore," Biff persisted as he pulled the blankets off John.

John grudgingly rolled out of bed and sluggishly put on his blue jeans, black T-shirt, black leather jacket and the black Beatle boots he had purchased from Shelly's of London on Oxford Street.

"Great!" Biff declared. "Let's go paint the

town red!"

I hope he doesn't mean that literally with blood, John thought.

Biff marched down Bayswater Street with John in tow. They jumped on the first red, double-decker bus they saw and hopped off in Soho.

They were trudging in circles trying to find some nightlife when they stumbled upon a queue in front of a nondescript club. Biff went ahead of the queue and tried to enter when a bouncer pulled him up.

"You'll have to wait in line, Sir," the black colossus advised in the most gentile manner, belying a physique that appeared as though it could unleash Herculean force.

Biff edged up to the bouncer, puffed out his chest and rose on his toes in an effort to stare him down.

John quickly moved alongside Biff and took him by the arm. "What are you doing?" he asked. "Just stand in line, it's not very long."

Biff continued to stare down the bouncer who was holding his ground, returning the stare with confident determination. Biff then cracked a smile and followed John into the line.

"Quite a nippy night tonight," Biff declared as condensation emanated from his breath as he exhaled and it mingled with the chilly air.

Biff approached various people in the queue in an effort to engage them in conversation, making a nuisance of himself.

The bouncer soon approached Biff. "Sir, please stay in line," he requested, again in the most polite manner.

"Oh, you want me to stand over there do you? Well what are you going to do if I stand here?" Biff asked tauntingly as he stood firm, right in front of the bouncer.

"I just asked you to stand in line, Sir," the bouncer explained. "And the line is over there."

"No! Why should I!" Biff barked back.

John quickly moved to Biff's side. "Settle

down Biff."

Biff ignored John and shouted at the bouncer. "Well. What are you going to do about it, gov?"

John was utterly frustrated and mumbled under his breath exasperatingly, "Gov? Now it's as if he's playing a scene out of the series *The Bill.*"

The people in line heard the comment and burst into laughter.

Biff and the bouncer were distracted by the noise. They both looked at the people, back to each other and then joined in the laughter.

John was surprised by the reaction but sensed that the digression had diffused the tense atmosphere. "Why don't we split this joint, Biff?" he posited. "I'm freezing my nuts off!"

They laughed as John pulled Biff away and they returned to the Park. Biff went to bed and, even though they had been sharing the room for months, it was the first time they had actually slept in the same room.

John was troubled by the events of the night but he went to bed and eventually managed to get some sound sleep.

Chapter 19

A Mystery Illness

The following week, John was going out for the evening to take a series of night camera shots around London.

"Can I come too?" asked Poppy.

"It's going to be a rushed job," John warned. "So I'll be on a very tight schedule."

"I know you're a slave to your plans," Poppy replied, "but I'm still keen to tag along."

John darted off and Poppy followed close behind. They rushed to the Underground and happened to just miss the train, so his first photograph was of the train leaving Notting Hill Gate Station.

The next train arrived and they resumed. John hit a cracking pace and Poppy was right beside him, both were exhilarated by the tempo.

Poppy was much more knowledgeable about the London transport system and often guided John towards the more appropriate route.

They were absolutely flying, rushing to the next stop and catching the most appropriate form of transport on the way.

John took pictures at the locations and at just the right angles, as he had rehearsed when he took the same photographs by day. He captured many night attractions, including Big Ben, the Lloyd's building, St Paul's Cathedral, Harrods, the Tower of London, Tower Bridge, Buckingham Palace and Piccadilly Circus.

They were having a great time until Poppy pulled up abruptly.

"Are you all right?" John asked

"I can't go on," Poppy replied.

"What's wrong?"

"I have to go pee."

"Oh okay, maybe you can go over here?" John queried.

"No, that's closed," Poppy advised.

"What about you try over there?"

"No," Poppy replied with resignation.

"Why not, is that one closed too?"

"No, I mean it's too late."

"Oh, I'm sorry Poppy."

*　　*　　*

John often reflected on that evening and how they shared emotions that ranged from exhilarating highs to an embarrassing low.

It was only a week later when John heard that Poppy was in hospital.

Rushing to the hospital, John bought a bouquet of roses on the way. "Hi Poppy, how are you feeling?"

"Pretty well, thanks John."

"You gave us all a bit of a scare."

"I gave myself a bit of a scare."

"So what's up?" John asked in a casual manner, attempting to disguise his concern.

"I don't really want to talk about it."

There were a few moments of silence before John spoke. "So when do you think they'll let you out of here?"

"I'm not sure," Poppy replied.

"Well, you'll have to get better quick and get back to the Park," John suggested. "Harold is dying to see you."

Poppy put on a wry smile. "Do you want me to get better or not?"

Chapter 20

Leaving London

John sought to find out what was wrong with Poppy but no-one seemed to know the nature of her illness.

Poppy returned to the Park and was feeling better, although John sensed that she was a different person. She wasn't as carefree and she appeared to lack her previous usual frivolity. These characteristics seemingly gave way to a new maturity and an almost constant seriousness.

*   *   *

Con returned from his tour of Ireland and Scotland ahead of his departure to Greece. He stayed at a bed-and-breakfast and visited the people at the Park every day.

Con was conspicuously quiet about his tour, being very evasive and abrupt in his responses to any questions.

John sensed that something must have gone amiss and suspected that Con had probably clashed with the other passengers on the tour, but he did not press Con about it.

John submitted his notice at work and the staff gave him a send-off, bestowing upon him a gift of a diary for his onward travels.

After three months in London, a lot had happened and John was feeling physically and mentally exhausted.

Thursday 16 June 1988 was the date John was to depart for his "Grand World Adventure" tour. His friends at the Park assembled around to see him off, although Con failed to make an appearance.

John said goodbye to Poppy and Lizzie,

giving them both kisses on their cheeks. He then bid farewell to Marty and Harold, shaking their hands.

John had a strange feeling as he made his way to Notting Hill Gate Station.

Catching the train, John travelled to Russell Square Station and scrambled his way to the Royal National Hotel—the meeting place for his tour's departure.

People were milling around a tour bus and John joined them.

"Okay everyone, please board the bus after you've loaded your bags," the tour guide called out.

The bus made its way to the port of Dover to connect with their ferry-crossing to France.

Gazing out of the bus window, John saw his life during his time in London flashing before his eyes. He was unsure whether he would ever see his friends at the Park again, but what he was sure about was that it was the end of an era.

Chapter 21

Returning Home

Con returned to work in Australia a month earlier than planned. Other workers noticed a change in him, which was manifested by his aloofness and a social phobia which seemed to have developed into extreme introversion.

John returned to work on Monday 12 September 1988, after six months away. He enjoyed an exhilarating world tour, which he was excited to talk about with his co-workers, although Con always avoided the gatherings.

John tried to reconnect with Con, but was

completely ignored. He then attempted to confront him by bailing him up in the cafeteria.

"Con, why don't you talk to me?" John asked, but Con didn't say anything and tried to bypass him. "Con, what's wrong?"

Con was ducking and weaving, trying to get by, but John placed his body in front of him and didn't let him pass.

All of a sudden, Con emitted a loud scream, "Ahhhh!"

John was horrified, signified by his wide-eyed and open-mouthed expression. He immediately turned his body to let Con through.

John was traumatised by the incident, which prompted him to approach Con's manager, Milton Ward.

Milton was a mature-aged gentleman who was widely respected. He practised due process, but was also a practical man who exhibited extraordinarily good judgement.

"I was wondering how Con was getting

on?" John asked Milton.

"As a manager, I usually keep information concerning my staff confidential. However, I'm well aware that you have been Con's closest friend," Milton stated at the outset.

"Con seems to be struggling since he's returned from leave," Milton continued. "Even though he's had strong familial socialization, he has always had a broader social phobia and his overseas experience seems to have exacerbated his condition. He was encouraged to seek medical advice and has been diagnosed with social anxiety disorder, whereby he is undergoing cognitive-behavioural therapy. As much as Con has had your friendship in the past, he definitely needs you friendship now."

John nodded as he reflected on what Milton had told him.

Undertaking extensive research into the condition, John sought out information in an effort to ascertain how he could best help Con.

There was a quite a bit of information on the condition and John sought to summarise the most important aspects into some easy-to-remember points:

- Encourage social engagement.
- Be friendly, but not pushy.
- Be a good listener.
- Be positive and don't criticise.
- Be patient and not demanding.
- Be alert to the warning signs.
- Encourage ongoing treatment.
- Learn and share information.
- Be there for them and be supportive.

Over the next several weeks, Con and John slowly opened up lines of communication with casual conversations.

At times, Con was prepared to divulge what was plaguing him. "I was stuck with relatives who I didn't know and who I couldn't communicate with," Con explained. "They only spoke Greek, you know."

"I guess that would be difficult for anyone," John said, trying to be understanding.

"I hung around the house a little while but I couldn't handle it, so I walked to the beach every day where I sat on the sand, looked out to the ocean and listened to the waves," Con revealed.

John stayed silent, living the experience vicariously.

"It got to the point when I feared getting out of bed and having to face the relatives," Con said and took a moment to reflect. "So one day, I got up early, before anyone else got up, and just left."

"You just left, without letting them know?"

"Yeah."

"I see."

Epilogue

John kept in contact with Poppy, Lizzie and Marty. He had no immediate plans to travel overseas, but he hoped that he may see them again one day.

Over the ensuing months, John managed to regain some of Con's trust and they conversed, albeit on an irregular and infrequent basis.

John did his best to support Con and to be there for him, although they failed to re-establish the friendship they once had.